The Bickersons'

Love Letters

by John & Blanche
Bickerson

Edited by Ben Ohmart

The Bickersons' Love Letters
© 2010 BearManor Media. All Rights Reserved.

Published in the USA by:
BearManor Media
PO Box 1129
Duncan, Oklahoma 73534-1129
www.bearmanormedia.com

ISBN 978-1-59393-534-4

Printed in the United States of America.
Book design by Brian Pearce | Red Jacket Press

An Editor's Note

For those few of you who have never heard of The Bickersons or read their rather incredibly eclectic book, *The Bickersons' Guide to Marriage*, the following may come as a bit of a surprise to you: they were a couple in love. Deeply, and without deviation. Only the hardships of finances and sleep habits prevailed to make their peculiar pairing historic and bitingly infamous. Here is the story of one passionate man who loved a woman perhaps too much, and she, him. Theirs was a mixed marriage — man and woman — that tested the theories of: environmental influence, and can too many cooks spoil the garbage? Left to their own world, perhaps John and Blanche Bickerson could have remained the boringly unaverage ideal couple. As stocks fall and unemployment bites man's leg, so too, do monetary woes capsize the Bickersons' lovey-dovey experiment.

Luckily for us, there is a testament to this amazing man and wife, from A to zzzzz. Little was known of the origin of this unfortunate couple; how they met, their backgrounds, why they fell in love in the first place. But, thanks to a fortunate bit of fate, we have nearly the whole story before us.

Jules Bickerson, only son to the famous fighters, was born late: 1960. Blanche was 44 and John was past dead at 43. Said Jules to this author, "I think my mom had me as a last ditch to get Pop to stop snoring. She figured as long as she was going to be awake every night, she might as well have a kid to bottle." Of course, she also assumed it would bring some much needed union to their sorely lacking union, when, in fact, it made life nearly the same crapshoot as before. John would drop dead a mere 15 years later, reportedly with a smile on his face, either due to his exceptionally white teeth (thanks to his brand of sensitive bourbon toothpaste), or the fact that he knew he was getting that permanent, lone vacation *finally*.

Being a patient fan of the Bickersons case as reported in *Psychotic*

Monthly (issue #313) and their globally documented story, I tracked Jules down, himself in the throes of a painfully messy divorce. Forced to sell everything he ever owned for a down payment on his first alimony payment, Jules, a slight man with a bent back and wide, penetrating blue eyes, reached into the garbage that day and sold me his parents' life story, via these letters, for whatever I had in my wallet that day.

The accompanying story of his parents' last days, told over toast and gales of scotch, is not for printing, as it has no basis in reality. Unless we are prepared to believe that Blanche finally murdered her husband because Captain Caveman had raised the price of hats beyond thermonuclear control. It's more probable to assume that Jules' crushing breakup he was then enduring was pickling his mind past preserving.

The letters, all handwritten in pink ink (Blanche) and pencil (John), are an amazing testimony to the most resilient married couple the world has ever known. Rather well-preserved, considering they had been sitting in the garbage for several years (not thrown out, said Jules, for sentimental reasons regarding *all* that garbage), the pages were of mixed quality paper and easily discernable even from the blank backs. Blanche's notes were crafted on egg-white, heavier stock paper, written in various shades of the aforementioned pink ink (yes, apparently there are multi-shades), with hearts over the i's and a small petaled flower within any capital D, O, P, R and hovering in C's. After which she folded the pages into cute animal shapes before inserting them into envelopes. Whereas John's businesslike strikes of dull, bold pencil cut deep into his choice of cheap paper, often cutting *through* whatever stationary he could get his hands on (furniture store, diner, Presidential hopeful, etc.) and ripping right through some of his more fiery passages.

These passionate exchanges evolve through the entire time of their meeting, dating and marriage, finally passing into passion of a different nature, as you shall see. Always there is strength between these two. Like an alligator against a gorilla. Who wins? Who knows!

Ben Ohmart

The Bickersons'

Love Letters

April 4, 1936

Dear Ms. Peaches,

I know we just met and perhaps writing to you like this seems — presumptuous. But I just wanted to let you know how much I enjoyed our dance together. I'd like to see more of you. Would you please accompany me to the drugstore where it would be my heart's delight to buy you any sort of ice cream and nuts?

Your ardent admirer,

John Henry Bickerson

April 5, 1936

Dear Johnny,

What a lovely little letter! Please call me Blanche. I love the way it falls off your tongue because you don't have any kind of accent at all! I would be delirious and delighted to accompany you, as you so dashingly put it, to the drugstore for an amazing dessert! I can't wait!

Please ring my bell at 6 this evening and please don't bring me flowers. Your sweet smile smells plenty.

Warmest regards,

Your Blanche

April 7, 1936

My Darling Blanche,

I feel as if I'm walking on air, my sweet, only powered by the wind of your smile, the brightness of your collar button nose. Ever since the end of the film, when I squeezed both your hands and said goodbye, I have felt a sense of peace and complete calm, only augmented by sublime and supreme happiness. I cannot believe my good fortune at having met you, my darling. I hope you don't mind me calling you that. I believe you are.

The Good Fairy is now my favorite film. It is *our* film now, darling. My arm still goes numb when I think of sitting with you in the dark theater. Reaching for the same piece of popcorn. Looking at you. Missing the middle 23 minutes just looking at you.

You move me to poetry, Blanche. I'm sorry if it seems too much, too soon, but you have awakened the dapper cry of Keats and Poe from my gushing heart. I want to bemoan to the world what you mean to my interior.

O, the cry of the ship of the squirrel in dark's hearth quiver
Undying naked flee upon fudge gouging deeply
Love leaning, sped mank, dank, envelopes thither
Where passions pass past perhaps seeded heatedly

Lore, darling, expectorates your long midnight hair
Shirted, trite, abysmal to facelessnessless apart
Kiss hands, understand, I am, to your impassioned affair
All that golden, wooden, fete, ever only light but dark

That, my dear, is from the bottom of my blissful soul. Until next we meet, I remain,

J

April 8, 1936

Dearest Johnny,

How distant last Tuesday seems already when we met at the hop. I loved the Hong Kong theme, and you looked so lovely as a geisha. I know you said the style was really Japanese, and female, but you looked so *cute*. And I really admired your courage, Johnny. All these boys today trying to look so cool and proud and what British royalty calls "butch," and everyone on the right side of the room dressed almost identically in samurai costumes. And you there with your long skirt and sticks in your hair. And powder puff face. Why, you weren't trying to look cool at *all*. You were *so cute!*

You had the eye of all us girls, Johnny. You must've seen us all, staring, whispering. Every girl there wanted to dance with you. And you came right over and chose me. Me!

It was the greatest, greatest dance of my life, Johnny. I was floating. Floating! It was the first time I ever got to lead. I thought it was so sweet that you wanted to remain in character. I really admire that kind of…manliness. You have real command. Confidence! You don't care what others think. I don't care what you think either! You're my one and only this week, darling John.

I will call you John, I think. If you don't mind. You are so manly and important. You are my John.

Your B

April 8, 1936

Lovely B,

I had to run out and buy a new pen because of you. I gladly did so, so I could answer you personally, immediately, because I could not wait, my darling. It is all I can do to contain myself not to contract in this passionate missive.

You have given my heart wings, sweetest of sweethearts, and I can see it winging out the window *now*. Towards you. And where you live! Never in my 24 years of life have I been this happy. I wish you were here to *pinch* me *now*. I have seen a *dream* walking, and it is you. Are you walking after my winging heart, darling?

April 10, 1936

Dearest Blanche,
Where are you??
Your own John

April 11, 1936

Dear John (and a *good* Dear John letter it is!),

Here I am! I'm so sorry, darling. I'm afraid I got hold of some day old dating advice and applied it long after it went bad (how's that for poetic! You are rubbing off on me, darling!). I asked my friend Gloria Wince — you met her at the dance — you called her loose legs because of her stockings — what I should do about you, silly boy! since we talk so often on the phone. "Should I stop writing him letters?" I asked. "Because we talk for at least an hour, sometimes hours of an evening!"

Well, I won't tell you her "official" advice, but, rest assured, she is now stricken off my Christmas list, darling, because I would never hurt you or ignore you by post for *anything*.

Your last, short note hurt me deeply, John. I did not mean to disappear. Not after our amazing, terrific trip down Memory Lane at Dirk's Carnival! What a wonder! I'd never been on a "car ride" ride like that before, where if you don't step on the gas and use your turning signal, the car doesn't even move. What fun!

And it was so nice of you to let me pay for the evening. You were so sweet and shy the way you asked me for the money to try to win but lost that *beautiful* pink yellow labrador retriever dog that would've been *wonderful* to bring home. I'll *always* remember it hanging there, darling.

I like a man who understands the value of a dollar and borrows it so seriously and boldly. I really respect you, John Bickerson. I know you work hard at your hard working job, and I know my parents are going to think that, too. I like a man who sweats. It shows that you are daring, darling, and not afraid to get your head wet.

I will always treasure that 3-leaf clover you found for me growing up between the cracks in the parking lot. It was the sweetest, most romantic gesture anyone has ever done for me. I love the way you kissed it before wiping it off and giving it to me with that grand, royal bow you had. The smile in your mouth and eyes is like my photograph of romance. You are my prince and I — well, you'll have to wait and find out!

Your ever faithful —
Blanche

April 15, 1936

Dear Ever Faithful,

I am reading your letter again as I write this. You said on the phone many, many times that you love my poetry. Now if only I can get you to say that about me, I can be an insane man! So, until that time comes, my pet, I serenade you with...

Person with flowers, my love is
Soaking in esoteric hours, my love is
Wearing gods' perfume, my love is
Greater beauty than moon, my love is

I buy the stars, the moon, the scent, the flowers
I rent her love, her loving eyes by the hours
I store a chiseler's enthralled statue in my heart
of a thing of a beauty, my Blanche, my art

Be with me
Need with me
See with me
Stay with me
Hey, with me
Shall we sail on life's stormy sea
together, forever, you and I

I have never been so moved to write poetry to any other lady I have known. Until you, Blanche, my soul has been without words. I've never used the dictionary so much in my life! It really is an *amazing* book. Full of words and adj., adv. I wonder what they mean.

I'm really looking forward to Saturday night. I have a surprise for you. Something that sounds cute. Just like your big button nose.

Until the weekend, Blanche, I remain yours,
John B.

April 23, 1936

Dear Blanche,

I'm *so* sorry about what happened. I'll never be able to forgive myself. Can you ever forgive me?? I know you have, through your voice, many times, dear Blanche, but there's something about seeing it in writing that makes it so…legal. Final. Please say you do, my darling!

But how fortunate you were able to catch that bowling ball in time. I'm glad we agree that it's much better to have a broken hand than a broken foot. I've never seen anyone dive quicker to pluck a bowling ball from the air like you did, darling. You are *amazing!* Such quickness of spirit and agility of thought! I've told the story to everyone who wasn't there and everyone is so impressed with the way you were able to stop it from crunching my foot *and* keep the foam on the beer. You must really love me, my darling. I will, too. I mean, I must also.

That's why it's perfectly okay if you can't write for a while. I understand completely. Even though it's not your writing hand that busted. Still, eating with your left all this time, it must tire your one appendage considerably. You are my heroine! And I am thoroughly addicted…

Now you just sit back and let me do some of the work, darling. This seems like the perfect time to tell you more about myself. It seems like we're so busy living in the present, having fun with popcorn and talking about when we'll have our first kiss, that there's never time for anything of the past. Except when you talk about your old boyfriends. Which is so cute.

Okay, here goes! Well, as you know, or might have guessed, I come from a broken home. My father up and ran away with a traveling saleswoman one day. They met when he just opened the door one day, and there she was. Many, many open doors later, my mother wondered why the heating bill was *so* high. When he wasn't around to pay it any longer, she knew.

And she came down hard on the old man, always complaining about the way he chewed his sweet potato pie and ran off with women. How he was always wearing *too* much plaid and running off with anyone with a Fuller brush.

Sorry, must dash!

J!

April 25, 1936

Dearest Darling,

I'm again so *sorry*!!! But it was for your benefit. The last post was being collected as I was writing, and I had to chase Mr. Bluit down the sidewalk right after I told you about my dad's plaid!

I desperately wanted you to have something to read during those long, cold nights we've been having. And I'm sorry I haven't been able to call recently, but the telephone company has been having a telephone shortage lately and I had to give them mine until they curb the crisis. It shouldn't be long now.

I understand how tired you've been lately, what with Ralph *[Blanche's dog – ED.]* up and running around too much after he got painted "flaming pink" by accident. Such a shame.

Anyway, next in our John Bickerson saga…! So, growing up with just a mother around was an interesting experience. I was born and raised in Plain State, New Jersey and I think that's where I got a penchant for the cold. Even to this day it's very difficult for me to catch a cold. I go out without my shirt in the snow in the street and everything and I just can't seem to catch one! Still, it keeps me working.

I was fair to genius in high school, but Lead *[as in "pencil" – ED.]* Science was my best subject. Straight B grades. We had an abundance of very special specialty classes in Plain State Public. Introductory Glue was another interesting excursion which I was rather adept at. I could stick anything to anything and you'd be surprised how many girls there were in that class!

Alas, I did not care for grades too much, and no one really told me how important they were to the welfare of one's later life because of scholarships. Someone *had* told me about *welfare*, however, so I thought I was safe.

I was a big baby with a chronic calcium deficiency in my toenails, which turned them solid white. There. Now you know why I keep my feet covered in church.

Well, that's a costly ailment, so between that and my mother having next to nothing in the bank, I started going around with a mock street gang on my days off (which was frequently, in those days) called The Yella Fellas. It was a name that picked up more fights than girls. Our burlap jackets had to be painted black freshly daily, but that summer sun played mighty havoc with that plan, so pretty soon we took to just going out in our undershirts, showing off our muscles. The only thing was that we were going into stores to steal food for our starving families, and without those bulky jackets to hide the goods, a lot of us got caught with the booty stuffed down our shorts. It was lucky that I looked young enough and the owner's daughter of the main store we trod in smiled at me more than once, so I tried, but I was never convicted.

I tried to join the Army during my last year of high school, because the government is good about those monthly checks, and my mother was eager for that. But they wouldn't take me because of my flat feet, wavy hair and contrary attitude. Mother was crying, in her clam chowder every night. And that's why I never order it when *we* go to a pizza place, darling, because I've had enough watered down clam chowder to last me a lifetime.

And that led me to a slow, unsure world of retail jobs that pay less than poverty. Just before we met, I was an usher at an all-night movie house, but I just couldn't stomach the mush and shoe gum. Oh, how I think of John Barrymore differently now! You have turned me into a simpering, elongated bundle of emotions not fit for the rattle in a fool's bell stick, my darling, darling Blanche.

I am changed. Touched. Moved. I think I'm going to call you right now!!

J

April 27, 1936

My own Blanche —

How time flies when you think you are in love! Wings of angels, shoulders of unicorns, soles of Mercury and Vulcan, I see them all in my sleep, my love, surrounded by your face, in a blur of whirl-wind motion, poetry spilling from my filling like rhyming, blinding unreason!

My apologies for the words, but when you have found perfection, words are the only toys a mere man as myself can use to construct what is a concept far greater than myself. I have seen God in your smile and my mind has to adjust through mere human concepts, or else rage with the impossibility of dreaming in absurd theory that cannot comprehend the mere meaning of — gorgeousness!

Yours in love and your own,
John

April 30, 1936

John,

These past days have been Super! I can't believe what a lucky girl I am, darling. Your constant calls are really scaring my mother, but you have no idea how healed I'm getting just by knowing there is someone wonderful out there thinking of me. I read your letters several times a day now — all of them — and I know I'm not supposed to tell you that, but I've been told I have a simple mind, so I don't really know how to be subtle. So — Write More! I love it!

And, dear John, I think I might love you.

Now that my hand is healing and it's only partially curved *[X-rays showed no real visible deformity – ED.]*, I'm going to return your lovely favor and tell you some of my history, because you need to know how *much* your words have done for me, beautiful, darling, darling John.

Well, as you will soon know, my parents are a typist and a doctor. I'm their only child so they tell me they spoil me terribly, but I really don't feel it. It's a wonderful shock to get everything you want all the time, but it really hasn't changed me at all.

I really like birds and pink, above all things, I guess. Except for you, dear! I didn't really like school because history was incredibly boring and exercise class was mostly outside in the summertime. I don't remember a lot more from it. I graduated, I remembered that. My friends all went out on a yacht on that graduation night, and Jill, she used to go with Norman *[No idea – ED.]*, she had to bring all her dogs with her because she had an afterschool dog walking service and it was just very embarrassing.

I'm not really good at this, now that I think about it. I've been sitting here for 20 minutes trying to think of things. Do you really want to hear all this?

Your lovely Peaches

May 5, 1936

My Dear Blanche,

I haven't heard from you for two days. I've called, but someone I assume to be your mother always answers the phone. She really sounds like you. A lot like you.

Are you ignoring me, Blanche? Is that really you?

Do you hate me because of the strawberries?

Your John?

May 7, 1936

John, John, darling,

No, no, you must never think anything you do bothers me. That really *was* my mother who answered the phone. But I had no idea you were calling! She never told me! In fact, after I got your last letter, I asked her about it and we really fought hard about it. I don't think she likes you, John. She said something about dog meat and your name and something about pineapple and disappointment. I couldn't understand most of what she said because she started crying, which made me start crying. She started pounding the pavement after she fell and really started pouring her heart out. It's too bad I couldn't understand any of it, because it was really passionate and reminded me of you, John. Very passionate.

I know it doesn't seem like it, but I sat here for five minutes trying not to use the word passionate again, in this letter, but I just don't have your intelligence, darling. You'll have to be the brains in the couple. I'm always so impressed when you make the man at the movies believe that you're a secret service agent by flashing that cereal badge you keep in your wallet. I like that wallet, honey, but it's kind of wearing thin. I can see how much money you've got without ever opening it up. So don't be surprised if you get a surprise for your next birthday!

Love,

Blanche

May 11, 1936

Dearest, lovely, incredible, amazing, special Blanche,

How I love your birthday present! I couldn't believe it! I still can't!! I never thought our first kiss would be like that. Me with my eyes closed under the tree, you with your knee on my neck, the bees on my feet, and you smiling and laughing with the honey jar.

It was the most romantic thing I've ever known in my life!!!!! When you pressed your lips to mine, and mine parted with sweet anticipation. A kiss that lasted eons. What Einstein has said of the universe has not even done justice to the arbitrary incredulousness of my satisfied anticipation of this miraculous event!

Sin of desire, flower of might
Rove me a table full of sprytes
Full to your neck, lips lusting inch
Blanche's light nature, like a finch

Sparkling, dazzling firework POOF!
Given my eyes and feet once aloof
A power beyond mere heaven's trod
My heart's peaceful sinking like a cod

The memory of our first kiss, darling, which will haunt me *forever*, gave instant rise to the poetry I had to shed from my soul, dear, dear darling. I sincerely hope you did not mind. I can't forget it. I will never forget it. I own it. You own it. Now that it has passed from you to me: the best birthday present a man in love can achieve. Thank you, sweetheart, from the bottom of my cells.

The leopard-pattern socks were nice, too. Thanks.

Your man,

John B.

May 15, 1936

Dear John,

I didn't have time to call, so please say you'll come over at 7 on Thursday so you and I can meet my parents.

I also had to tell you how *much* I enjoyed our very original date last night. I've never been pine needle picking. I've built snowmen before, when my parents and I visited Norway that summer, but building a pine needle man in the park was such an original idea! You're so smart about those things, John.

Oh, and I never did answer you. Of course I don't blame you about the strawberries. I thought it was a very romantic gesture to offer us to go picking strawberries in that woman's garden. Just because she wasn't romantic, that's not your fault.

Love,
Your Woman

May 22, 1936

Dear John,

I felt like there has been something cool between us for a while now, and sometimes it's easier for me to write my feelings down than come out and tell you. So, forgive me, John. But I have to ask. Are you upset with me?

Your Sensitive Girl,
Blanche

May 24, 1936

Blanche,

No, no, darling, why would I be upset? I was only humiliated in front of your parents, that's all. Why should that bother me? I have no soul! So what?

I'm sorry, darling. Like you, I put a lot of time between this paragraph and my last. I thought and thought and I wish I could start this letter again, but it's my last sheet of paper and I'm beginning to fear the ink in my pen won't last.

I'm sorry for what I said in that first line. Nothing's wrong. Yes, I'll admit I was upset before. But not with you! And certainly not with your *lovely* mother. Your wonderful dad who knows the *power* of a hard working man. *Delightful* people!!

Your beautiful mother — what a cook! I have never, ever had before cactus soup, but I've always wondered what it might taste like. And that eggloaf was *something* else. Imagine having something half scrambled and half fried! With just a hint of sage and more than a clue of boiled beef broth and tarragon. There was one taste I just couldn't fathom, my love, and I wondered if it could have been detergent? I must admit my smile looked whiter than usual when I brushed my teeth that night.

I swallowed every bite with a smile, my love. If you can cook half as good as your mother, Blanche, that will be something *else*.

But I have to admit I was a *little* intimidated when the questioning came.

Postman, sorry!

J

May 24 and a half, 1936

Sorry, honey,

That guy seems to sneak up on me earlier and earlier every day. Anyway, I'm writing this as I watch the postman walk away from my window view. I know the garbage cans are just outside, but it's either open the window for fresh air or stick with the stuff I've got in here.

Anyway, I was talking about question time. Your parents really love you, Blanche. But I feel like I had Black Death stamped on my collar. It was colder than a penguin in there, honey. Your dad ceased to be impressed with my job, though I told him I'm lucky to be working in these trying times. He didn't seem to think that picking up trash that the prisoners miss is true work. He should get out there on a hot August day and see if it's anything like lounging around the south of France!

I'm sorry again, sweetheart. I went and made myself a Swiss on Italian and the last cool beer to calm down. Just the thought of losing you when your parents...might not think I'm good enough for their princess! How that fills me with vampire horror! The thought of losing you —!

It was too much to bear. I had to go and lie down for three hours. I know it seems strange telling you these things. You can't see me sleeping with agog. You don't know how long these terrible letters of mine take to construct, like I've yanked out my fingernails and write with my oozing blood. You can't see the anguish with which I write with such *passion*.

I should stop now. I love you, darling.

Your John

May 26, 1936

Dearest John,

I'm really, really sorry I had to break our date last night. I've been having trouble with my father who really seems to hate you, John. I don't know why. You are the most wonderful man in the world! Hard working with the soul and the mind of a poet, but whenever I tell him these things, he tells me he has to go get the car washed. Why do you think that is, John?

I really admire the way you work with your hands. Daddy thinks that means you should be able to build ships or something. Do you think you could build a ship, John? That would really go a long way with proving yourself to him. Or maybe you could just discover something, like another continent or, I don't know. I've been sitting here trying to think how to continue that last sentence. Do you think there might be any more continents? Or maybe some long island, in a place with *good* weather? That would be nice. Finders keepers, and we could build a house there.

I like it when you open a tough mayonnaise jar. But when I tell Daddy your wonderful qualities, he talks about rewooding the floor of the yacht in November.

I cried, really hard. Mommy sat me down and showed me her wedding album. The pictures were mostly dark and scary. All the men were tall with black hats and I thought I saw Lincoln once, but she said it was some old dead tree. She pointed to dead Uncle Herman who was a planter, who married my beautiful Aunt Merfurd. He was honest as the day's long, Mommy said, and Uncle Herman worked himself to death planting those marigolds, and it just didn't pay off. I think she was trying to say that being with you would mean a life of hardship and damnation, but she didn't *say* that. I think she really likes you, John. Because then we visited her Hope chest which is only a couple miles from here, buried in the woods near a dam. There are dead apple trees nearby. I never understood why she kept her Hope buried. Inside that was her wedding dress, which had blood on it, and her wooden wedding shoes. She sighed as she showed me these things, plus fifty thousand dollars in cash.

That was all that happened. I thought she was going to tell me a story or something, because she did seem romantic. But she was shut up pretty much the whole time. That must mean that she really *likes* you, John, because she imitated — is that the right word? — that the Hope chest was mine. Maybe a wedding present?

I'm glad you like Mommy's cooking, darling, because she's taught me everything she knows. But I have to admit — I think I'm more creative than she is! Just wait until you try my eggplant basil sundae. You won't believe your stomach!

So don't worry about my parents, John. They would argue with me a lot if they thought I was ruining my life. And they're not doing that yet. They've always tried to protect me. I don't mean like they think you are a burglar or something, but maybe stealing me away? Anyway, I'm a little over 21 now and I'm going to love you and do what I want, darling. My parents will understand. Even if it kills you.

Love,
BP

June 5, 1936

Dear Blanche,

I don't know what you said to your father, but where I am is amazing!! *[Peru, Indiana –* ED.*]* They have everything here! I honestly never thought there was a school that taught how to subscribe to magazines, but you should see the size of these entrance halls!

See you soon!
John

June 8, 1936

Dear? John?

Your letter was so short! Now that you're in college are you forgetting about me? Don't tell me you're surrounded by all those young students in the short pants and ponytails, wiggling their fingers at you. I'll just die! And don't say you're too busy meeting people and going to parties to sit down and end your letter with love or something I can really cry over because I'll just die! Why don't you get up out of that girl's lap and call me, John!

Crying Blanche!

June 11, 1936

Dearest Lovely Blanche,

I'm so sorry you had to wait for this missive, but you should know that I didn't bring any nickels up here with me to make a telephone call! Your father gave me barely enough for bus fare. I had to hock one of my silver fillings just to make up the difference!

Apparently he thinks it's enough that I'm here and that he's helping, that he thinks I have ambition enough for going halfsies on my education. Well, taking a class on how to fill in a *form* is past ridiculous and I'm going to tell him so when I see him!

Yours,
John

June 11, 1936

Dear Blanche,
Ignore last letter.
Hot headed John

June 11, 1936

Dearest Lovely Blanche

I'm so sorry you had to wait for this missive, but you should know that I didn't bring any nickels up here with me to make a telephone call! Your father gave me barely enough for bus fair. I had to hock one of my silver fillings just to make up the difference!

Apparently he thinks its enough that I'm here and that he's helping; that he thinks I have ambition enough for going halfsies on my education. Well, taking a class on how to fill in a _form_ is past ridiculous and I'm going to tell him so when I see him!

Yours.
John

June 22, 1936

Dear Blanche,

Okay, stop ignoring me. I've learned my lesson! I *need* to hear from you! I need to hear your phone. I need to hear your voice in a letter that I read over and over at night as I sit in my lonely dorm room among the homework and distant sounds of lonely guitar from the other inmates.

I never knew such a course could be so long! So intensive! I always thought all you had to do was fill out the form, and the magazine would start to come soon after, but there's so much *more* to it than that! Choosing the pen, writing in block letters — and we've had *lots* of practice on E and A! — then there's the psychology class in which we try to match up the subscription to the sociological individual, finding the kind of mind that will read each magazine. So I have to intensify my brain in another sociology course on how neighborhoods and genes both affect the personalities of kids being raised today. So complex! And to think I used to think it was just writing your name and address on a card and sending it in. We've got a pop quiz coming up soon on the correct usage of the return address!

But I sure appreciate how much your father wants to help us. Blanche, with his help, I know I can make a go at this. You watch! I'll be a doctor before you know it! Frankly, I always thought it had more to do with going to medical school for nine years. But if this is how your father started, you can bet I'm going to subscribe to his footsteps!!

Your ambitious,

John

August 18, 1936

Darling,

Your nightly calls have kept me going. I think I would go mad without them! You said you wanted another letter from me, and here it is. I'm sorry it took so long, but I have been quite reflective lately since this is my last week at magazine subscribing college and I can't believe I'll soon be in your arms again. I need you, too.

The kids here are a swell bunch of form fillers; one of them is a prodigy! And we've got some guys who look like they're in their 60s, but boy, can they keep up. One of them got a B on his last paper. I'll admit I hated it here when I first came, and that's why my grades suffered, because I didn't apply myself early on, getting D's. And then with your help and spiritual guidance, I found myself wanting to succeed — for us. So this last month I got straight A's. Yes, I'm serious. Yes, I know you already know it, but now it's written down. *Here*, in a letter. *Straight A's*, Blanche!! Even though I now have a C average, but I've passed, darling! That's what counts. And I'm coming home to my love.

Anyway, a bunch of us kids are going out tonight, probably after our telephone talk. We're going to wear paper hats and drink sassafras. It's going to get pretty wild. But my only thought will be that you won't be here.

William *[No idea – ED.]* sends his love and kisses, and I told him I was going to take a percentage of that first! I hope your father will be as proud of me as I am. He's getting a real professional in his office, I have to tell you. The course of unbending magazine corners was intense, but I came out *first* in the class! I think it's my knees. I can stay crouched quite a long period of time, and my pounce when someone first lays the magazine back on the table is like a tiger, dear! My fervor is what's tops.

Seeing you soon!
John

August 19, 1936

Come home to me, John.

You have a fervor? You never mentioned it in our talk tonight. I do worry so for you, John. Have you met many pretty girls at college? I worry about them, too. Mostly I worry about what will happen to you if you meet many of them.

Who is the youngest person you've met? I don't mean that prodigy, but I looked him up. That's great that you should have someone so young interested in Mozart in your class. But I'm curious about the women there, darling. Have you found anyone as pretty as me yet?

How hard have you been looking? I haven't looked at all here. Gog Bersen did ask me out last Friday, because he said I was pining for you. He said going out might take my mind off you, which I thought was nice of him. We didn't do much except went to that local fair that you and I went to a couple times. But he drove us to Dixie instead of waiting for it to come here. I tried to get him to take my share to pay, but he was so *stubborn*, John. Not like you!

We played rollerball and pitch-the-milk cans and I had to wait almost 20 minutes for him by the kissing booth where his sister was performing. It was embarrassing. I had worn my cotton candy down to the nub and I just stood there like a tourist. He was so red when he returned, embarrassed himself, I expect.

He tried to hold my hand in the tunnel of love, but I slapped his face good with my corndog. Can you imagine that? Where it was dark and all! What if I had fallen out? He's no gentleman. Not like you, John. You were so nervous when you asked to hold my hand, the right one, I thought you were going to faint! And after I said yes and you woke up, your hand was so cold and damp. You were so gallant. And you hummed that Mexican song about cockroaches while you rubbed my wrist. It was so romantic. You said my hand smelled just like garlic. I'm eating garlic right now, my love, thinking of you.

After the tunnel, that's when I had Gog take me home, right after he bought me that stuffed pony. The one I sent you for your aunt's birthday. How is she now? Is she still alive?

I'm enclosing a picture of me in my newest French bikini, so you'll have something to show all the girls!

Your lovely,
Blanche

August 24, 1936

Dearest Blanche Honey,
I've been telling you how wonderful things are lately, on the phone, because I'm afraid of upsetting your parents when you cry. Well, if you've never done this kind of work, you won't know how hard it is to keep your self-respect, but I'm going to try to tell you anyway.

Blanche, honey, you *know* I love your folks, and for all the good things they're doing for us. But I just can't breathe in that office! And it's not because of the fresh paint. Whoever heard of black painted walls in a doctor's waiting room! And there I am, standing there in a dark suit, waiting for someone to put down the magazine so I can go straighten it. Unbend the corners! These magazines are *not* costly to a man of your father's wealth, Blanche. Besides, if they get ruined, aren't I a college man? With the diplomaed ability to subscribe to yet more of these crummy paper time wasters if I need to? These people read for all of two minutes! I swear, I've never seen a bigger collection of people who get someplace earlier than these idiots. They don't want to read! I swear they're more interested in getting in there for some uninterrupted *pain* than seeing the latest mountain in *National Geographic!!!*

Okay, I've calmed down. My neighbor, Dot Plantagenat, came over with a misdirected package. Believe it or not, the thing had my name and address on it but I never ordered it. Well, I learned long ago not to say no when the mailman delivers. You never know, you might get something good. Well, this was a bottle. Something called bourbon. I had a taste of it just now. And it really calmed my hair back down flat.

Blanche, darling, I just don't think I'm cut out for the doctor's office life. I'll stick with it, because I love you. But I ask you: is keeping *Esquire* always at a 90-degree angle a sane job for a grown man?

Your man,
John

August 26, 1936

John —

If you love me, you'll keep going to work every day. Daddy says if you keep at it, you can take over for him some day. Oh, I would be so proud, to be the wife of a doctor, to be the wife of Dr. John Bickerson! Doesn't that sound lovely, darling? Then you could *really* put me under!

Your loving,
Blanche

August 26, 1936

John ~

If you love me, you'll keep going to work every day. Daddy says if you keep at it, you can take over for him someday. Oh, I would be so proud, to be the wife of a doctor, to be the wife of Dr. John Bickerson! Doesn't that sound lovely, darling? Then you could really put me under!

Your loving,
Blanche

August 28, 1936

Blanche,
Darling,
My Love,
My Own,
Don't you understand what it takes to be a doctor? It takes years of medical school. Training and training. You're up at 5, you take classes in basic anatomy, basic Latin, you attend countless lectures of bone structure (the leg bone's connected to the hip bone, etc.). All kinds of biology classes. Hours and endless days of study, and that's not even counting learning how to cut people open, and waiting all the tables it's going to take to pay your way through *all* those years.

How do you expect me to inherit *all* of that — all of that — from your father? Blanche, answer me that. How do I suddenly get all of that mighty knowledge by standing between the rubber plants waiting for the sound of bending paper? Answer me that!

Your incredulous,
John

P.S. I was a *fool* to think you started in the *waiting* room! Blinded by love! Hours and hours of standing!

August 30, 1936

Dear John,
Oh, you're so smart. I love the way you talk in your letters. You're such a smart man, I know you'll figure it out.

September is almost here, darling. Remember what we talked about? Can we?

[No sig. Weird. – ED.]

September 1, 1936

Sigh,

Yes, we'll go to the beach. I'll pack up the cooler with some coconuts and green peppers and a few magazines if we get bored and let's just go out and get CRAZY. I'm ready for it!!

Giving up to your love,

John

September 7, 1936

John!

I know I just left you and I know it was perfect and I know you *know* it was perfect, but I couldn't let my head hit the pillow on our first night back without telling you how much I *love* you.

Love you.

I love you!!

Darling, this week was PERFECT.

I'm going to sleep tonight with that bottle of white sand you collected for me with your own toes, under my pillow, darling, where I will hear the sea in my dreams. And see the sea again. I don't know where you found purple sand, but it certainly is quite a mixture!

I've never caught and ate my own snails before. I felt like I was in Paris! I never knew they could run so *fast* either. What a day that was!

How are your legs, darling? Have you been able to get all the sand out of your arm hair, too? I thought it was so sweet of you to let those children bury you like that. You were so popular! I think I counted almost twenty children by the time it was up to your chin. They were so artistic. Did you know that they wrote "For Sale – $25" on your chest when they finished? I'm sorry again, darling, but I really thought you could breathe under there. They certainly *seemed* to know what they were doing.

I think one of the things I like most about you, John, is your generous nature. No sooner had the reverend dug you out than you were trying to reward them with "wuffer." Are those like wafers, darling? *[What John actually said was that he was going to give the kids "what for" – ED.]* My uncle Mike used to make "iron bar" candy bars when I was a tiny baby. And they were especially for prisoners. Wasn't that nice of him? It took a lot of chocolate.

Well, let's get back to YOU. *You* are the man of my dreams. I've been to the best restaurants in London and Missouri and Peru, India, Australia, but I don't think I've ever been to as *wonderful* a place as Ed's. Wow, what an elegant experience that was. And all because of *you*, John. Making it so romantic. I shall dream of that tonight. And the image of your face covered in wet sand!

Loving you,
Blanche

September 9, 1936

Dear Blanche,
It was good seeing you again. Our date last night underneath the sink was a true testament to our strong, immobile bond between us. How unlike other women you are that you don't mind having a date by a dripping faucet bathed in candlelight. Of course, I wish I could have taken you out properly, but a job's a job, and if I'm going to save up for that special present for you, well, I really appreciate your attitude. Not many girls would split a carton of sesame chicken under the pipes while getting dripped on the forehead. You're a real trooper, Blanche! I found those candles in the garbage, by the by. Just goes to show you what people *will* waste.

Your lovely,
John

P.S. I meant "you're lovely," sorry.

[This letter was probably misdated, understandable in Blanche's frenetic mood at the time. Obviously, it relates to slightly earlier in their relationship when John was away at Magazine College. — ED.]

September 10, 1936

John,

Honestly, I don't like it when you compare me to the other women in your life. I know I'm not the first, but I don't need to be the last, I need to be the present. Do you understand? I have cried myself to sleep the last five nights after getting your hurtful letter comparing me to the tramps you've known. And I've burned it! I have feelings, John! You have felt them, you know!

At first I was so happy about our beach trip. Recalling all the sand in your shoes and that cute little way you complained about everything. Everything except me, of course! I still have that starfish you murdered for me as we got on the bus going home. I wish I could remember the poem you said as last rites, but I can't. Could you write that for me again? I miss your handsome poetry.

Perhaps you're saving it for your other girlfriends. Like that Gloria Thipsaw, the one across the hall from you. Why do you have to live in a female dormitory, John? I still don't understand the reason for that. You told me, but your explanation is so fast, so complex. Why don't you write me some more poetry? If it's because you don't love me, that's fine.

But if you need more inspiration — you didn't used to, with my beauty and figure and all that you said — but if you need it, how about starting with this line?

"Blanche, darling, you're more beautiful than all the women of the world…"

I hope that helps. I didn't do very well in English class, but Daddy says I'm going to Harvard in a couple of years. You know I took time off after high school to see the world. It was a nice place.

Do love me, John. Say it. Say it, darling!!

Your broken hearted Blanche!!!

[Same here, for some reason. – ED.]

September 12, 1936

Blanche, darling, you're more beautiful than
all women of the world
The way the sun kisses your amazing blonde curls
Even with hair so straight, it's true
I was under the gun for a rhyme, what can you do?

Your eyes are like the ocean
Your teeth as white as clams
Your feet give me the notion
What a lucky, John, man

If ever I break your soft, pink heart
I know shall I surely die
Blanche, my love, let us not be apart
Else my pencil shall surely sigh

John Bickerson

[Okay, now they seem to be back in the present, so I don't know what she was talking about before. It does seem clear, however, from John's previous letters that he had had enough of the doctor's office and had quit. Or had he? Perhaps he had taken a second job? It seems unlikely. But the man was pathological. – ED.]

September 13, 1936

Dear John,
   That was pretty good. I have left your sweet words under my pillow. Because I want to feel them creeping into my mind so I can believe them. I liked our telephone talk tonight. I just wish I could see you more. I've asked Daddy about giving you more time off, but he says this is the busy season. Don't people get sick all year, darling? I know the work you do is important, but you can't be *that* tired when you

come home from standing in the corner all day, can you?

I forgot to tell you that I saw old Mrs. Hubbert yesterday. She had an appointment with you and she wanted me to tell you what a lovely young man you are. So respectful. She likes the way you hold your hands together in front of you, looking up at the ceiling all that time. She says you have wonderful hearing, the way you can tell if she's put a magazine down even though you're looking up. And I told *her* that I'm very proud of you, John. Mrs. Hubbert says when you take over the business, she won't take her corns to anyone other than you. Isn't that wonderful, darling? Your first customer!

Thank you for the poem. I hope the next time you can send me something with more lines in it. I read that Byron wrote his *Inferno* as a whole book. A poem the size of a book! I wish you could write me that much romantic poetry, John. I've heard a rumor that there's a dictionary of rhymes somewhere that really takes the guess work out of finding the right rhyme for writing to your lover. If it would help you write a whole book for me, I'll buy you one for Christmas, my love.

Where would you like to go out next? I want to pay this time. I won't even *hear* of going Dutch again! Where should we go?

Yours in love,
Peaches!

September 15, 1936

Dear John!
Where are you? No calls, no letters! What happened? Don't you still love me? Please answer me or I'll go out of my mind!!!!
Love?
B??

[The following exchange of four letters is probably in correct order. There seems to be a missing section of letters since John and Blanche probably communicated mainly by phone during this period. There is quite a lot of unexplained detail within their undated exchanges, but this is mainly due to John's sudden knowledge of erasers. He never used them before this

point, wanting instead to scratch out and start again, else the muse of his passion burn out during second thoughts. – ED.]

[Undated]

Dear John,
The only way back is forward. Isn't that what Jill *[Who knows – ED.]* says? She might be right. The tree is a little darker now, and the leaves are still there. My theory is that it's not a Christmas tree, because that has pine needles, doesn't it?

I put pressure on it today, and I only screamed and bled for 90 seconds this time. I'm looking at a box of crackers because on the front yellow box cover is a picture of an anteater and it somehow calms me. I have no idea why an anteater is supposed to sell crackers. It isn't even cute.

I still can't believe we survived that. It's funny how good crackers taste to me now. But I told you — even having something simple to sustain me was my ultimate goal. It became my religion and your god. It was so cute the way you got down on your knees to pray every night. I just wish you didn't keep muttering to yourself, because my pastor says a prayer is God's words, and you shouldn't mumble them. But I forgive you now. Whatever you said to Him worked. It was like a miracle — it *was* a miracle! And you were his tool.

I'm still exhausted. I'm going in to bed. That's funny. I just looked and that's where I've always been.

Say you love me, John, and I'll be the happiest woman in the world.

Your ScuzVum,
Blanche

[Undated, but obviously following the previous]

Blanche!
You remembered! I know it was something strange to call you when I was dying of thirst and food and boredom, yet, I meant it with all my heart, my ScuzVum. It was the first thing out of my mouth. I'm glad it only took two hours to explain that I meant it with all my

love. You were exhausted and so was I. We hadn't eaten for 45 hours. Tempers would, of course, be high, my languid love. But everything is fine now, and we are ourselves again.

I love you.

You love me.

How happy we will be?

Actually, the way I think of it, this will be something to tell our grandchildren about. To look back on and laugh during our comfortable evenings at home. Already a smile is plastering my face just thinking on it!

Your hap-happy John

[Undated, except for the number 303 in the corner written in what seems like blood]

John!

Our grandchildren! Oh, this is so wonderful and so sudden! Yes, let's think about our time on the water now! And often! If it causes you to think of marriage and grandchildren, yes, let's think of our wonderful memories that began as terror! I'm doing it now, John!!

Loving you,

Bl

[A mustard stain is all that dates this one. – ED.]

Blanche,

I mean my dearest Blanche,

Well, I didn't *really* say anything about marriage, if you recall. But that doesn't mean I'm against the idea. Some of my closest friends have committed *[to? – ED.]* marriage. I think we're both still suffering from island fever or whatever it is you get on boats. I mean, it was almost a week before they found us. Frankly, I'm still starving to death, and by now I think I've eaten a whole buffalo. I never cared for plain tap water before, but I think I'm really getting into the stuff now. It's magic!

And if it wasn't for that simple trip to Coney Island, with my darling, I would not know today the simple pleasure of just a glass of water. Just like you and the crackers, my love. All it takes is one slip up to send us somehow from the tunnel of love into the ocean — I still don't know how it happened — starving together. *[Apparently, their boat somehow got dislodged from the usual Tunnel of Love tracks and their impossibly tight hooks and veered into deep-sea water, without anyone at the kiddie park or the Coast Guard or ships in general catching wise. These boats were not designed for non-coastal waters, so it's incredible that the couple survived at all. — ED.]* Only our love and raw pike to keep us strong.

I could still smell the hot dogs. I still remember you shivering in my arms, my darling. No water, no popcorn. Just the thread off my buttons and your hat pin for catching our daily bread. Hours and hours and hours of searching the seas for that one little nibble. No radio. Nothing to look at except the constant up and down and your darling little head over the side. My poor Blanche. How you suffered! But you were right, you were a much better fisherman than I. Oh, how I wish I had a camera — you and that 8 lb. sea bass! Skinning it with your teeth. Boning it for me. What a newsreel that'd make!

And yet. Through all that. There was a little piece of me. Just a small particle that wasn't starving or as cold as space, that never wanted us to be rescued. Alone together, forever. The smell of you and pike and sea bass. The view of you in my arms and a sunset. Isn't this the address of heaven? It isn't next door!

Your man,

John

P.S. You put the wo! in woman, you do.

[Note: Dates are on the rest of the correspondence, except for a few amazingly saved greeting cards years later. Why the above exchange was undated and somewhat stained is unknown. I made an uneducated guess as to where to stick these letters and as far as the narrative goes, I believe the choice was a wise one. Though no other letter from here on refers to their incredible seafaring incident. — ED.]

December 12, 1936

Dear Blanche,

This is just a quick note to let you know I lost your Christmas list. I mistakenly wrapped some fish in it because it was the longest piece of paper I had and Chauncey *[John's boss at the fish market, on the edge of the Lime River, for which he was currently working. – ED.]* won't let me unwrap the hake. I sincerely hope you kept a copy. It seems like such a lot of work to dash off without backups!

Loving you,
John

December 12, 1936

John, my Love,

I hope you got this in time, sweetheart. You sounded so desperate! Yes, of course, I kept a copy. In fact, I made 7 copies, so don't worry if you have to wrap fish in this one, too. I really admire what you're doing for us. If I had to work three jobs — even one job! — I think I'd go crazy. I don't know how you do it. Are you sleeping at all? We've been together almost every night this month so I know you're not doing anything for at least three hours a night.

I know you must be exhausted, working so much before Christmas, so I've decided that I'm going to sing to you on the phone next time you call. Think about what you want to hear. I want to practice and make sure I know all the words. Not Christmas songs. Those are *old*. We're going to sing those together anyway. But please don't make it too hard like last time, ok? I never even heard of Sir Francis Bacon, never mind that he was a songwriter. You're just so intellectual. But I'm a simple princess!

My love goes to YOU!!!
Blanche

December 15, 1936

Dearest Darling,

I'm sorry this took so long. My fingers have been cold lately. I had to start cutting the tips off the fingers in my gloves to do all the watch repair work. *[John's second job during this time was repairing watches for Jacob Marley Resorts. Apparently it was the only hotel in the state where, while you slept, you could get your watch fixed at the same time you had your shoes shined and hair washed. – ED.]* The trouble is, the old miser keeps the place deathly cold. Oh sure, he'll turn the heat up when a customer complains, and with a smile! But if we say anything, even if we blow into our hands within eyeshot of a customer, we get the whip. Later on, I mean. Too bad he pays so well.

My hands hurt, but I wanted to write this down. Did I ever tell you about the first Christmas I remember? I must've been six. My mother had made the eggnog correctly and she was swishing it down like a washing machine. She was seeing a real heel who made shoe racks. She didn't see the heel in him, not then. He was going bald and tan, but that one Christmas, for whatever reason, he gave me the best present I think I ever had in my life. Even wrapped it. I guess he really wanted to make an impression with me, the kid, and he did. Five bucks!

I couldn't believe it! I'd never seen that much money, not all in one place, and not made out of paper. He told me to run out in the freezing snow and get whatever I wanted. I did that! You don't just tell a kid that and then watch him stand there.

I ran out in the freezing cold and was promptly hit by an ambulance. As they put me on the stretcher and put me in the back, I could see the five bucks fall right out of my pocket. And into the snow. I never saw it again.

But I often think about that five bucks and what might have been.

My entire life might have been different.

I got you a present. My hint to you:

It cost more than five bucks.

Because I love you,

Darling!

December 17, 1936

John, my John,

Your story of your missing money moved me to tears. Now I know what to get you for Christmas. I won't tell you, of course, but you're going to love it. I've been pulling my brains out trying to think of what would make you the happiest boy in the world. Now I know.

Let me tell you what Daddy and I did today. Well, he bought me a skating rink! I couldn't believe it! And I've never skated in my life! I can't wait for you and I to go on it. I hope I don't fall through. My ankles have been getting a little fat lately. But I've heard that when you skate, you can make snow cone ice, shaved, and you scoop it right up after you've skated, flavored and everything! That's why the one we'll be shaking on looks brown. Cola flavor!

Daddy said he was going to wait for Christmas, but he had no idea how to wrap a rink, so he just told me as we were going to get ice cream. I put fudge on mine.

When we were talking, Daddy told me again he'd like to have you back in the office. He said no one turns a page like you, dear. He didn't actually use the word "dear," that's from me. You know, thinking about it, I feel a bit warm and lightheaded right now. I hope my letter makes sense to you today. I think it's all the excitement. Mom got me a diamond necklace for Christmas, you see. I saw the receipt fall out of her sable at the table and she didn't see it or see me pick it up, so I quickly stuffed it into my shoe. I didn't want to ruin the surprise.

Have you ever been ice skating, John? I know you don't like the cold because of that time you got locked in the freezer by an Austrian person *[No idea – ED.]*, but it seems like when you're skating, unless you fall, you aren't really going to be cold all over like you're in the freezer. You're floating and laughing and I'd think by the time the cold gets to your waist, it's melted by then. Your ears and hair should be fine, I mean.

I hope you can hold me up like those Olympic people do. That looks like fun! I know you have strong arms, from shoveling that coal last summer, and driving that heavy garbage truck last week. You shouldn't have a problem at all with petite little me. I told you how much I weighed that time you got me drunk. Add on about 10 pounds for clothes and think about it, John. I'd love to ride high in the air and

I'm sorry, I have to stop. I can't think of anymore. I don't think it's the receipt really. I think that baked fish we had before the ice cream was strange. My mind feels all woobly. All the time it took me to find woobly in the dictionary! It's not there!

I'm going now. If you love me, get me princess skates, darling!
Blan

December 19, 1936

Well, Blanche,
You've shot Christmas right from under me. Not only have I been slaving like an Egyptian for the past two lifetimes, but I've already bought your three Christmas presents! And now you want skates?? Just because DADDY buys you something to run them on?
Come on, Blan!!!
Disgusted,
John

December 20, 1936

John!
I don't mind you getting upset, but why do you have to wait two days to do it! We're supposed to be happy and in love this week! This is Christmas, John! The time of fellowship and good to Amen! Don't ruin it by being a jealous spoilsport!
I'm sorry I said that, dear.
But I believe you owe me an apology. And until I'm right, I can't have a good Christmas with you, John.
Your obedient,
Blanche

December 21, 1936

Blanche,
Okay, look. Maybe I flew off the handle a little, but can't you just consider *my* feelings for once time in your life? I worked like a dog

with no nose and a broken back to purchase the Christmas trinkets you asked for. That list! And I got you 3 in the top 10 too!

No <u>thank you</u>?

No *sorry*?

No nothing? For all that toil, all that sweat? I swear I'm three inches shorter from the fire I burned under and four inches taller than that working up the calluses on my feet from taking on that fourth part-time job digging shells out of the gratings in the peanut factory. What is a day off? I don't know! I've denied myself sleep and kingdom come so you could have that faux jeweled pink pill box you so desperately wanted at Sam Macy's Apt. Store.

And all the other stuff? The genuine popped popcorn holder with the adjustable fork handle? I should apologize for suffering famine and sunstroke to buy you these treasures that are forgotten, like a child, when Daddy's big head buys you a new bag of jacks?

Are you *insane*, woman?

Silently,

<u>John!!</u>

February 12, 1937

Dear John,

I couldn't believe it! How sweet!

Yours blushingly,

Blanchey

[If there were letters written between Christmas and the eve of Valentine's Day, they would tell quite a story. There is no evidence the two ever wrote over this time period. How they made up from the previous tiff is a mystery all married men might wish to be privy to. However, their only son offered this puzzling clue to this editor: "I do know that a homeless man who had been paid two bottles of hooch to play Santa accidentally burned down that ice rink before either Bickerson had a chance to skate on it. I still don't know how you burn down an ice rink, but I guess once the hot dog stand went, it just couldn't be saved. Or wasn't profitable to keep it going. Perhaps it was a tax write-off for Grandpa." It may have been that once

the object of argument had been dealt with, love once again reigned down upon the Bickersons and they were too busy making up to take up pencil and pink pen again, for a while. One can only surmise. – ED.]

February 14, 1937

Dearest, most darlingest Blanchey,

This is your V-day letter, my love. In it contains all my worldly awe. My half-closed eyes' inspiration for seeing you and dreaming you simultaneously. The poetry is in my soul and it is dripping like water out, out into the sea of your beauty, as far away as New Zealand.

These past however longs have been the best odd number of months I've ever known. To see time pass in a vacuum with no course, with no wind, just moving along, head over my heels, enveloped in a power far greater than myself: there is no more sobering realization than such incredulity.

You are my Earth. The place from which I was born, the place to which I shall always belong. Dust to dust, John to Blanche. A man's home, you, dear. In cold, sweat, sleet, tornadoes, bad tomatoes, and tropical nights, you are where I hang my hat and beat the dirt off my shoes at night.

You are my Journey. I know not where it leads, but you take me there, up off my mind, my troubles. When I see myself falling, I know it is towards you. When I beam with an uplifting gait, I know you are the cause and the treat. You are the inch of shoe leather off this mortal coal, gaining in time and spirit, making me age, but accepting the fact that with each step comes a greater love, more than I ever know or admire. You are the first-class ticket, the passage on a warm fairy as it sprays the sea at me, you are an ocean liner and a car with the top down, ignoring street signs, going faster and faster and anywhere and everywhere, darling.

You are my Song. The words bred by poets, the music chopped into urgent melodies and popular tunes filling up faces with only the most pleasing of oompahs. And deedle doos.

I have no right to look at your face. Nor kiss your large hand. Nor do I expect to keep on living just because God has blessed me with such an item of exquisite beauty and gainly temperament; luxury, as if the stars had carved out perfection and sent it beaming to my own world, of who I am, the ideal I should always be. I should be struck down with fast moving lightning, crashing into my unworthy shoes like a THUD! in the night, the dog I am, daring to look into the light that is your hair, your face, your perfect sprite of a figure. Your true, heavy, amazing, testing, vacuous, incredulous soul.

If this letter is a true measure of my love, it cannot be measured, it should be never ending and powerful, yet the powerless, lifeless thing it is, is nothing compared to the black spot in my heart that is fear, doubt, loathing that you will one day realize that I am nothing and leave this nothing that I am.

You would take my life.

You would crush my hope, my spirit. Spit on my shoes and wipe them with your stare.

I am all that is yours, darling Blanche. MY darling Blanche. Dare I call you such!

And on the holiest of Love Days, this St. Valentine's Day, marred by history with a celebrated killing spree, as that which celebrates true love and true lovers who forsake all others for each other. This small collection of words strung together by love and fear — fear that you will someday leave — is, I hope, the smallest spec of one percent worthy of your eyes reading this paper. To validate my true feelings through merely the mind writing on this page is my quest, and hopefully you see it straightfully, unblinded by the care I believe you have for me.

Say you love me, and I believe that quest has reached its conclusion.

Say you need me, and I will someday die a happy and unbroken lover.

Say you want me, and you can have the other two. The smile on my broken lips, beaten by thugs, ripped apart by starving sharks, my toes emptied of their nails and hair, the hair on my head waxed and burned on a slow spit, all of these and the devil's map of tortures more will my smile shine teeth to the heavens if I hear such words from you,

Darling Blanche
My Love
My Own
My My

John

February 14, 1937

Dearest John!

Oh, how I loved your incredible letter! I shall treasure it always! But I'm afraid it arrived opened, because the present or chocolate you must have sent inside didn't arrive.

See you in three hours!

Your lovey,

B

February 15, 1937

Dear John,

I really think you're being unreasonable. I don't like it when I call and you pretend to be an operator. I know what your voice sounds like at a high pitch. Don't you remember that time you screamed so much when we went up in that Ferris wheel on that windy day? I remember that tone, and I think it's rude for you to try that on your sweetheart.

I'm still your sweetheart, right, John?

I'm sorry. I didn't understand when we were watching the movie [The Good Fairy *again. – ED.]* that you were in a bad mood at *all.* I'm sorry, okay? But you didn't have to scream at me about that letter. I told you it was a very Good letter. Really long and smart and all. Some of it I didn't understand, so I called up this girl who's in college, but I really couldn't understand what she said either because of all the laughing. I just couldn't help laughing.

I'm sorry, John. I didn't realize this was your present. You said that it took you a long time and there's more thought that goes into this than buying a diamond ring, but really, I don't mind if you're thoughtless sometimes. A girlfriend of mine was dating this sailor once, and she took him to dinner one time at Madame's *[A swanky restaurant in Harlem, NY where marinated fish went for $1.98 per foot. – ED.]* and he got down on one knee after the crab cakes and opened this pill box which had the biggest diamond ring she had ever *seen* — and she's seen a lot, John. She was so happy and cried so much, and he tried to calm her down by saying that it wasn't much, he'd just seen it in a window as he was passing and thought she'd like it. They didn't get married because it was a friendship diamond, she said.

So you see, you don't have to put a lot of thought into things. Even if you want to copy a page of Shakespair for me, that's fine. The important thing is that you love me.

You do still love me, don't you, darling?

Yours ever fretful,

Blanche

[According to their son, Jules Bickerson, the rift between his not-quite-yet parents went on for a number of weeks because of this incident. John had broken his back, probably figuratively, at a job in a cement doorstop making factory, in which he would have to move stock from the molds to the trucks and constantly keep an eye on the batter to make sure everything was free from dead mobsters. He had been saving up for the possibility of marriage, which he thought would take a lot out of him, financially. Because of this his nerves were frayed and he was growing weary of filling the wants and desires of a woman who seemed to give nothing back.

"Dad definitely had a feminine side," explained Jules in 1997 over his usual coffee and fags breakfast, "as you can tell from all that poetry. I didn't understand half of it, and Mom would not re-read it, but she'd count the number of words the second or 22nd time she looked at his letters, comparing it to how many words were in the next *letter, like she was trying to figure out if he was beginning to love her less. It was funny to see her with that solar calculator."*

If Blanche had been receptive to putting back some of the affection she took, perhaps her response to this important Valentine's Day letter would not have signaled the beginning of the end of their pre-marital bliss. – ED.]

March 4, 1937

Dear Mr. Bickerson,

You've been so mean to me lately that I wonder if we should keep going out. Except for "Watch your head" when you opened the door of the *[Treehouse]* restaurant *[located in an actual tree, which required physical prowess to get into; only the strongest tasted their cheap steaks. – ED.]*, you hadn't said a word to me all night last night. And the night before as we walked along that damp stream you claim to be a river, all you did was grunt all night. I thought I was dating a baboon.

I didn't want to tell you this, but Herb Flobstitz has been trying to ask me out for the past two months, and I kept putting him off. I thought you and I were going to be together always!! I don't know anything anymore. Should I go out with him, John? I get so lonely when we're on dates together. I can't keep up the conversations by myself, you know. Sometimes I just don't know what to say to myself. Sometimes I ask a question, and I don't know how to answer!

Come back to me, John! Or should I go somewhere else?
Heartbroken,
Blanche

[Undated, but obviously the follow-up – ED.]

Herb Flobstitz!
Herb Flobstitz, Blanche? Is that how you want to go through your life? The wife of a *Flobstitz*? I don't even think you'll be able to say it without tripping your tongue over the piano stool. "Hello, I'm Mrs. *Flobstitz*!" After a couple staggers of gin you'd be hard pressed to say *that* in front of any preacher!

Go ahead, be a *Flobstitz!* See if I care! But if you figuratively walk out that door, Blanche, don't you ever bother coming back, do you hear me?
Defiantly!
John!!!

March 10, 1937

John!
How can you be so horrid! After all the time we've spent together! How many times have we gone to the park and watched the ducks? How many times, John?
Blanche!

March 11, 1937

Blanche!
What do I care from ducks!
John

P.S. Why don't you include some stamps once in a while!

March 12, 1937

Dear John,
I can't believe my beautiful poetic John Bickerson can be so cruel.
How is this possible, John?
Blanche

April 1, 1938

John!
Where are you?? Don't you love me anymore?? If you really loved
me like you said, you would prove it! What about a ring, John?
Your heartbroken Blanche

April 4, 1938

John,
When I asked for a ring, I meant more than just a phone call.
I'm going out with Herb tomorrow night.
Enclosed find your previous ring, the one I won for you at the
ring toss game 4 months ago. I don't want it anymore.
Goodbye.
Blanche

April 11, 1938

Dear Blanche,

I don't think I can stand this too much longer. You talk of heart-ache, and what have you done to me? I saw you out with a *Flobstitz* just last night and it cut me to the quick! I amused myself for a few minutes with that pained expression on your face when you suffered his picking his teeth with a pencil. And then erasing it, starting again.

But I couldn't enjoy your torment long, Blanche.

We need to talk.

John

April 13, 1938

Dear Blanche,

But we can't talk if you don't pick up the phone. I shall try for three more days, and then I'll assume you don't think our love is worth saving.

May you possibly be happy with a *Flobstitz*, if I don't hear from you.

Wandering John.

[*Herb Flobstitz's third wife, Seally, is still alive and recalls the sour nights she spent when Herb decided to reminisce about his previous rela-tionships. "Oh yes, I remember that Blanche. Always dressed in pink, he said, except for a couple of Friday nights when you see her out with that John Bickerson, way after they were an item again. She wore brilliant yellow dresses with black polka dots, and by brilliant I don't mean smart. She had these Eiffel Tower earrings she always wore, talking about how they were made out of Napoleon's bones, that her father got for her on the black market. Stupid woman. A charm and silly naive-ism in her personality. And she had beauty, but all on the outside.*

"Herb eventually became a dentist, after two years of law school, and he thought that Blanche was just the most worldly woman he'd ever met, all inherited from her father's trips, of course. That is, until Herb went out

of the country to learn about gums and learned more about women, so he had something to compare Blanche to. He fell in love with his first wife, an Australian, obviously named Sheila, and he came back and saw what a complaining brute was this Blanche. They went out a few more times, but Herb quickly saw that she wasn't worth the trouble. She said she was a $2.23 root beer in a $3 glass of beer. Whatever that meant." – ED.]

April 24, 1938

Dear Mr. Bickerson,
I'm ready to listen.
Blanche

April 30, 1938

Dear Blanche,
Thanks for talking with me. I'm really looking forward to our date tonight. I've been saving up all week, literally saving my pennies and dimes, to make this the most magnificent date in the history of dates, or at least ours. Darling.

Darling.

It is nice to be able to use that word again. I've felt so lonely without it. Without you. Not able to have the simple pleasure of just calling *YOU that* has been yards and miles past agony. Into the next state of Excruciating!

Here's to us. Tonight.
Love,
John

May 1, 1938
Dearest John,
I know now that it takes a strong man to love me. You have earned my trust, my darling. Now that I have known weaker men, you have no idea how much I appreciate you more.

My love!
Blanche

[John and Blanche had the biggest fight of their singlehood over the next two weeks, according to Jules. Or, perhaps one fight and a lengthy silence is more apt.

"The trouble with getting the story from Mom or Dad is that it changed depending on who told it. That's true of anything. And often, Dad was too drunk to remember his version. No, I take that back. I never saw my father drunk. He was like a sponge in the sink. Getting soaked didn't change his appearance; it just made him slower to wipe up his messes.

"Well, the argument probably began when they went to see A Day at the Races *and Dad neglected to open the door for Mom, who was pretty used to first class by then. Dad was dog tired earning the money for popcorn that night and even though it was only ten cents, Mom didn't really understand how much effort it took for him to buy her the lesser things in life. I loved her, because she was great to me. And the opposite to Dad. Funny, I never really looked down on her for that because I was a kid getting everything I wanted from life — why think bad thoughts against that person? By the time my mind was old enough to realize what she was doing to poor Dad, I was hooked on her with gratitude.*

"I do know that at the top of May Mom and Dad didn't talk at all. They didn't go out, call each other or write. They were both boiling, and both in agony, Mom later told me. Of course she also told me that Dad went on a cat kicking tour of New Zealand to forget her, during this time, so who knows what's true."

The letters that follow make no mention of this terrible row, or what caused them to get back together. But Jules gives one more clue as to that "agony" during this time.

"Mom gave up a first-class flight with her parents to trek through Angola during this time. They sensed she was completely miserable and tried to snap her out of it. I think she pleaded with Grandpa to give Dad his job back, but the office, I mean the waiting room, was full of books by then — classics like Frankenstein *and* The Frogs, *a Greek play — and he was pretty certain that Dad's training on just magazines wouldn't cut it in his upgraded waiting room. It was too bad.*

"And Dad meantime was checking out books from the library on suicide, so he said, but I sort of doubt that because I've never noticed anything like that in the New Age section." – ED.]

May 16, 1938

My darling,

I hope you like the towels. But I've noticed that the green actually rubs off, so please be careful. Also, it has a smell like freshly washed China — the dishes not the country — so if it's all too much for you, I'll understand if you want to throw them out.

Did you finish the book yet? I'm curious what you think. I think Twain is an amazing writer. But he can get a little fresh and intimidating, especially during all that football talk. Still, I told him it's good to get a woman's opinion. And who knows, maybe someday you'll see Blanche Peaches in the acknowledgement section of the new Dwain Twain book! He's going to be a bestselling author, I know it. There's never been a series of football books aimed at fairies and small children yet. Ask your father if he wants to invest in a small print run. Frankly I'd rather see Twain eat nails first, but I said I'd ask.

Now...on to love!

I want to take you to the swimming hole Friday. They said they needed something to plug it with. Ha, ha!

I'm joking! That's from Sam Taylor's joke book I just picked up from a customer two days ago. She didn't have a quarter to leave as a tip, I guess, and she left this book on the table instead. I read it while I wash dishes and it's given me hours and hours and hours of fun. Do you know: my dog has no nose? When I come over Friday, ask me how it smells. The dog.

I know I seem giddy today, darling, but that's what happens when you put your foot in a puddle of white paint and expect to curse the world, and what's on the bottom of your shoe? A five dollar bill! I couldn't believe it. Of course it took some vigorous washing to get the thing back to green so someone would take it, but those six hours of scrubbing really paid off, Blanche.

Yes, sir, I got myself a new suit — now I don't have to take you out in those old rags. Mine, I mean. And I got a hot meal inside me that had at least the *taste* of beef this time, with enough left over for a professional bath, new shoes, and a subscription to *Life*, which I've always dreamed about achieving. It's amazing how far a poor man can stretch a buck times five, eh?

You know, the girl who gave me that bath was amazing. Apparently

I've never done it correctly before in my life, and there were places it seems that had never been washed before! At least not since Mom died. I had a good and vigorous professional scrubbing that got some of the grease off from some of the last jobs I had. You should've seen her face fall after all that and I go and give her just a five cent tip. Well, I had to tell her what was what. Besides, I've been saving up my cash to buy you something, sweetheart, and no Asian dame with a sweet smile is going to talk me out of the other nickel.

See you soon.

Your John

May 20, 1938

Blanche:

The same to you and yours!

Furiated:

John!

May 21, 1938

Okay, darling,

I believe you. But what would you think if I paid a man top dollar to wash everything I had? Especially things that no one had seen before, and I proudly said he washed areas that had been untouched by human hands before? You would be livid, I know you!

That's all behind us now, darling. I forgive you. You forgive me. Let's kiss and make up.

Smootchy,

B

May 22, 1938

Dear Blanche:

I've been thinking a lot about our future together, dear. Well, our present too, of course. When you ran your bike into that dog last night, it got me thinking about how short time is and just how tightly our mortal coils are wound.

I've written you this little poem, because there are nights, like last night, when it's chilly and storming out, when I wonder about the shape of the world. It's still round, of course.

So is a busy *cannonball*.

Tidal earthquake tornafloodo and poisoned peach wine
Grisly ax forested in shopping, showcased smiled rocky highs
Love glue and barstools, you for me, me forecasting brown doom
Fruit on trees, money as leaves, ants inviting our picnics

Full stop, lemon drops and smashed bones in left legs
Letting Mother love you, crash, tramps, fools for us
How does a man live with sand in the eye, winking
At a savage Santa, all white, red from stark blood

It is the love, glues, forces, stands, needs, belongs
You are Elmer's, forces, stands, needs belongsssss

Do you see what I mean, darling? I can't live without you.
Yours in love,
John

May 23, 1938

Dearest John,

I really didn't understand a word of that. Thank you for not bringing up your poetry when we do fun things. You have an amazing mind, darling. I've always said so. But I might be the kind of girl who likes the kind of poetry that Hallmark likes. Now that must be some man. Mr. Hallmark can really turn a phrase, with rhymes and everything! You need to work on the ends of your sentences, John. I've heard that song lyrics are like poetry. They all sound alike at the end of their sentences too. And I remember in school, there was an old man named Byrod Keatesy who was always writing to women about very romantic things. That's what I like to hear, darling. Give me a tankard of that.

But keep being so intense. I like that. I think it drives my father crazy, when he sees your wild eyes, with your strong feminine black lashes, but I love them, darling. And wasn't it some poet who said the way to a soul is through its eyes? It wasn't the stomach, was it? I think that's really true, the eyes. You have such a cute soul, darling.

I've been wondering what we should do for the weekend. I hear there's a violinist in town performing at the Alsnowed *[Local vaudeville theatre –* ED.*]* and we can sit at the back row for just pennies. Actually, now that I've looked at the newspaper ad, I'm not so sure. He's advertised as "the violent violinist" and it seems he comes out into the audience while he's fiddling and strangles people, and depending on what seat you have, it depends on how violent he is. But it doesn't say if you get less violence or more violence for a cheap ticket. Anyway, it sounds like a hoot and I doubt he'll lay a finger on us with the seats we'll have. I would like a seat this time though, John. Standing Room Only is playing havoc with my figure.

I don't feel like sleeping just yet. So this letter is long. I think it might have something to do with your poetry. Sometimes it does keep me up. That one a few weeks ago *[It might have been an audio poem, read during a date. –* ED.*]* about the giant mashed potato attacking and killing all those rare birds really upset me, I have to say. I know you're sensitive and I'm sorry to talk about it, but I haven't been able to even put gravy on anything since that one. You have such a gentle soul, too.

Well, I'm going to try to go to bed now. I just looked under it and there's nothing there, so before it fills up with my fears, goodnight, sweet dear.

Your Blanche

May 26, 1928
I'm sorry, John.

[The above "letter" was obviously meant as 1938, and was paper-clipped to a piece of torn wallpaper. It may have followed a tirade from criticism of John's poetry. As Blanche correctly surmised, John Bickerson was a passionate, sensitive man with the spirit of a knife always trying to carve paper like it was wood. – ED.*]*

May 30, 1938

Dearest Blanche,

I know we haven't spoken much lately. I haven't been home much. I'm crafting this very missive in mostly dark, lit only by the lighter of a co-worker of mine here at Baileybay's *[A clothing store which catered to fat children. – ED.]* who is taking a little extra time off to go out back in the alley and eat the liver sandwich his cousin made for him. *Mr.* Baileybay says he won't have employees eating stuff in here that smells like that. Sometimes he and I trade sandwiches out back, and he wanted me to tell you that he adores your peanut butter and mayo on whole white.

In my horsebank *[A glass "piggy" bank Blanche bought John for their eleven month anniversary, which had supposedly been broken and glued back together by Richard II himself. – ED.]* I have literally been saving my dimes for you, darling. Regardless of money or food, every week for I don't know how long, and I've never told you this, I've been saving up to get you a special present, for the most special time I can think of.

That time is tonight, honey.

Your John

[The below was written on a greeting card which had the face of an old man and illustrated, swaying wheat for hair. His eyes were half closed, mouth gently parted. Inside was the simple word: "Thanks." Due to an uncertainty about the copyright of the strange drawing, I can't reprint said card here, but rest assured, it is spooky. – ED.]

June 1st [1938]

Oh my darling. What a wonderful gift. I shall treasure it always!
Blanche

[The above is probably a thank you card for the present for which John had long been saving: a pink duck for the bathtub that, when wet, also unfolded into a very smart shawl. The truth of the matter was far from the

above written evidence. It seems that the reality of the situation came out during a public 4th of June picnic in Wherever They Are, *a radio program celebrating the independence of America a month earlier due to* Wherever *freelance producers needing to sell the unsponsored show early; so, the program persuaded several small towns to have their fireworks a month ahead of time. Thor, New York, where the Bickersons lived, was one such conned town. According to documented, transcribed interviews with witnesses at the event, the realism went somewhat thusly in the tiny park that day:*

John: Beautiful day.

Blanche: It's a little chilly, isn't it?

John: My darling, just use your duck.

Blanche: What duck?

John: The shawl I got for you. Here, let me pour some water on you and we'll get it into shawl shape in no time.

Blanche: Oh, I don't have that dreadful thing here, John.

John: Dreadful?

Blanche: I mean, of course it's lovely, darling, but I wouldn't be caught dead in it. Then again, that might be fine.

John: But — the "thanks" card.

Blanche: I was just being polite, you know that.

John: I do?

Blanche: Of course! What woman would be caught dead wearing something like that?

John: Well *you* just said you'd be caught!

Blanche: Now don't get upset, John. It's a perfectly nice thought. I was just expecting something more…marvelous. Saving up your dimes.

John: I'm not even going to mention the nickels now.

Blanche: Oh, John! Another present?

John: It's past.

Blanche: What are you going to buy me, John?

John: Where is the duck, Blanche?

Blanche: Oh, that? I gave that to the neighbor's dog. I think he's using it for his bed. But they have to keep it wet.

John: A present bought with love!

Blanche: Oh come on, darling. It wasn't *that* wonderful. If you get me a diamond ring, I promise you I'd be crazy to give *that* away.

John: If I get you a diamond ring, I promise you *I'd* be crazy!

Blanche: Don't you *want* to give me a diamond ring?

John: Right now, I wouldn't give you the ring off a bathtub!

Blanche: How can you be so cruel?

John: I think it's contagious!

Blanche: What's that supposed to mean?

John: You're incapable of being satisfied! I try and I try and it's nothing doing! I give you the very stripes off my pajamas, and you're looking for polka dots. I gave you a good two-thirds of our last ice cream sundae and *nothin'*! No gratitude! Even the sprinkles! Didn't I get all creative and spend hours fixing you that grass sandwich in the park two weeks ago? Did you give me even the slightest wink of appreciation or "thank you"? No!

Blanche: I couldn't speak! I was bowled over after I found all those ladybugs in my teeth!

John: No, everything has t be *perfect* for Princess Blanche? You even turned up your nose at that painted box of Kleenex I made for you!

Blanche: Well you're not supposed to paint each tissue! I had blue up my nose!

John: And now I scrimp and go without cream in my milk for months to buy you that stupid duck, and the dog gets more out of it than I do!

Blanche: Why don't you get me a proper present for a change? I know you think you're "brilliant" giving me those embroidered rubber bands, but I don't know what to do with them!

John: It's *art*, Blanche, it's not good for anything!

Blanche: Don't scream at me…

John: I deny myself most things…I've been wearing my watch inside out so the sun doesn't wear it out. I paint my light bulbs yellow so I can buy lower watt ones. I eat my chili with a fork to make it *last* longer.

Blanche: And you buy your girlfriend cheap presents with the proceeds!

John: You must be a realist about the shape of the global economy!

Blanche: I could walk up to any man on the street and get a diamond ring from any of them!

John: What's the name of this street?

Blanche: Oh, don't be so funny. You don't think enough of me to buy me a flea collar.

John: I do too!

Blanche: Other girls are getting the good stuff. Look at Swahalia Shenbatt, the maid down the street. Just 21 and already she's got two glistening things on her.

John: Her boyfriend did that. Found out she was cleaning for *two* houses, if you get me, and pow!

Blanche: I wouldn't get you if you had measles!

John: Don't tempt me, Blanche! I'd go out right now and find a sick kid if I thought it'd do any good!

Blanche: Go! Get out of here! You don't really love me anyway! Other men have given me things! Shiny and precious things that go around my neck!

John: Well, that flea collar offer still stands.

Blanche: Oooooo, you think you're so smart! Barry Hockwater gave me the keys to his car once!

John: Where did you park it?

Blanche: I suppose all the girls in the neighborhood just go crazy for that dry wit!

John: As a matter of fact, they love the dry stuff!

Blanche: Well, most dogs prefer can food!

John: I remember one in particular! Her name was Parke Langer and what grand days we had on that red trampoline! So you watch yourself when you throw those names around, Blanche, because I'm all armed too!

Blanche: That's right, beat me! You've done everything else!

John: Not everything.

Blanche: I've never been so unhappy in my life!

John: What about last Thursday?

Blanche: I can't stand it, I can't stand it! Who is this Parke Longer?

John: Langer, Langer!

Blanche: You must've really loved her, you never mentioned her before.

John: Now what kind of correlation is that? She was just this girl I knew. I was eight years old at the time. Okay? There. I'm all out of animation. I mean ammunition.

Blanche: Did you really love her?

John: I was eight!

Blanche: You once said age doesn't matter in a relationship.

John: I don't believe this!

Blanche: I'm sorry, John. I can't compete with a memory like that. I'm afraid —

John: Like what? It was a red trampoline! One afternoon after school!

Blanche: I'm afraid I…have to break our steadyment. I'm sorry. I can't get over the way you've hurt me today. Here's most of your ring. The rest fell off a few weeks ago. Goodbye, John. My own…

[This public tirade was quite a remembered spectacle in Wherever *and soon claimed the attention of everyone in the park, including Sy Smit, a brilliant 79-year-old with a photographic memory, who soon after dictated the lively conversation to* The Paper, *the local paper. To most, it was the high point of the day, beating out the fireworks easily for spectacle and volume. – ED.]*

June 10, 1938

Where are you?

[The above was probably written by Blanche, but it's impossible to tell. The letter was dusted for fingerprints by this editor, but except for a telling smudge of lipstick on one corner, this was a very asexual communication. – ED.]

June 10, 1938

Dear John,

The last 40 minutes have been agony here. No visit. No phone call. What's happening to us? I'm beginning to think I'll never write again. I mean *you* will. Never. Oh, I'm just not good at these letters things. I'm all nervous about what to put down on paper. It if wasn't for the date sometimes, I think I'd go mad at these blank sheets staring at me.

You know, my mother never went out with a lot of boys when she was training to be a dairy farmer, she told me. She thought about her work and career and the cows every day, she said. I think I got her single purpose mind from her. I've seen the way she smoothes her dress out when she looks at my father. I want that kind of love, John! I want a life where birds are always singing in cages and dogs are running around the floor so much you trip over them. A *full* life. And I want it with you.

But it's been 50 minutes since you last called and I'm going out of my mind! I tried listening to Jack Benny but I can never get past his accent. I've tried reading a couple of those books you mentioned would improve my mind, the English language ones, but you're right, I need help on understanding the social structure of *Arms and the Man*. Plus, are you supposed to read all that dialogue out loud?

I love it when you read to me, especially in person with my head on your knee and the sky in your eyes. It's like I'm in the presence of a very smart god with nothing better to do. And I've been wracking my *brain* to think what I can do to give something back to you. It was my mother who gave me the idea. You'll be so surprised, darling!

Call!

Call!

I thought willing you to call would work, but it doesn't work after all, does it? I remember in high school, for my science project I watched a pot of water boil, and it really doesn't boil. I won't tell you what grade I got for that. It was my father's fault. But it was my idea to submit the same report to my psychology teacher when we had to write a paper there, and I got a B-!

Did you know that as an elective one year in high school, we got to take psychology? It was fascinating. Did you know that ducks have accents, depending on where they're raised? Just like people. And the human brain is big enough to process almost 50,000 garbage trucks. Something like that. Our minds are limitless. Except for my cousin Perel, of course.

Call!

Call!

It was worth another try. I'm just going to hang on until you call, or until I let my face fall flat asleep on the bed. I once stayed up over 20 hours, you know. My friend Leonard, you met her at the Three-

Piece Ice Cream Contest *[Sponsored by Blanche's father, so that he could give out free tongue depressors embossed with his street address. – ED.]*, she and I were talking about ribbons in our hair for that long. Our eyes were wide open and we were stuffing our faces with…something. But it smelled like chocolate. I think I got my sense of style from her. She was so fat she had *so* much style, using mostly black and pink and always looked at me to the side of her head, like a parrot. It was fun. She's a model now with long legs and diamonds and a castle and penguins in her bathtub that's shaped like a pool and cars, but I have you, John!

Don't I? Why don't you call?

Oh well. I'll use my time constructively, like you do, and prepare for tomorrow night's surprise. I'm even going to buy you a sleep shade so you won't know what hit you till the last minute!

Dream of me sweetly, and PICK UP THE PHONE!!

Your dreamgirl,

Me

June 12, 1938

Blanche, my dear!

What a night! I never knew you could be so romantic! I didn't want to take off the sleep shade after I sniffed what you had prepared for me. I've never been given a candlelight dinner like that — in — my — life!! The cinnamon-sugar veal appetizer. The glazed cucumber tea. The amazing striped chicken infested with lemon pork glaze! I didn't know which way to turn!

You really outdid yourself last night, darling. I don't think I've ever drunk so much in my life. Because — what was it? Rye? Bourbon? — it married so well with those nine courses. You know me, a Coca Cola is as wild as I get, but I just wanted to explain that I don't usually try to climb into a car with my fingernails like that. It was that food! It drove me crazy! I never thought I'd live to find out what gorilla tastes like! I'm impressed with how much hair you managed to get off that thing.

It was incredible, darling. The book-scented candles, I'd never heard of that. The florescent light near total darkness. The soft communist music in the background. It was a dreamily spent, well-thought out theme evening that I will *NEVER* forget.

I just had a few questions about the menu. A doctor friend of mine I was talking to was curious. That, uh, squid ball surprise. Just what was the surprise? That oak flavor? Also, we were talking and you were joking, I'm sure, but apparently there *is* an expiration date for blue cheese. Did you really get it from that car repair place on 4th Street?

Also, that salad was something else! Just what was it? I do like purple cabbage, but what were those blue chips in it that tasted like aspirin? I thought it was very daring of you, darling, to soak the entire thing in evaporated shrimp sauce. My doctor friend thinks you may have washed the romaine lettuce in a light detergent. Is he right?

I was so moved by dinner I know I didn't really touched the "lamb tainted sponge cake" you made from that parboiled flower substitute, but I'm really glad I took a portion home with me. It's still doing pretty well and doesn't seem to need refrigeration. I might take it for a walk one of these weekends.

So if you don't hear from me within the next couple days, don't worry. I'm staying with my friend. He's going to medical school right now but I'm going to sleep under the stars in his truck. I've always envied those with mobile homes. What do you think, Blanche?

Your loving,
John Bickerson

June 14, 1938

Oh John!
I'm SO so so so so so so so so so so so so so so so so so so so so so so so so so so so so so so so so so so so so so so so so so so so so so so so so so so so so so so so so so so so so so so so so so so so so so so SO so so so so so so so so so so so so so so so so so so SOOO so so so so soooo so so so so so HAPPY you liked my cooking!!! I was SO SO so so so so so so so so so so so so so so so so so so so nervous about it, as you can tell! I've never cooked for a man before! Mom gave me a lot of help and advice, and a few recipes, like that starting crab-mayo baked black bread appetizer. I remember how it bulged your eyes up something

so funny. Well, that may have been hers, darling, but the rest came out of my own head! I was so nervous, I just tried to keep it simple, but I may have overdone it. But now that I know you love it so much, I'm *really* going to pull out all the stops next time! Wait until you try my try my cheery fudge covered typewriter ribbon! Yes, it really *is* a delicacy in London! And —

But wait. We still have the sleep shade. I'm going to surprise you!!!

I simply live to please you, darling John.

My John.

I love you SO SO SO SO SO SO SO SO SO SO SO SO SO MUCH!!!!!!!!!!!!!!!!!!!!!!!!!!!!!!!!!!!

You know who!

[*It seems that John's sequel dinner was equally candle lit and filled with putrid dishes that only a man in love could tolerate. According to the Peaches' garbage collection agency, which had indeed made a note of June 17th's collection due to the exotic variety of sights and smells from that particular pickup, there were most probably creations made from soap, tissue, reeds (the kind a clarinet player might use), chicken necks, turkey spleens, hog's head butter, "ambient butternut squash dripping," pie of no visible certainty or odor, parson's nose and mustache, "baked liquid," filet of mother mouse, gizzards from unknown animals, and other items which they wrote in a secret code known only to garbage men, apparently.*

From witnesses we know that John armed himself with two bottles of hooch that night and three additional empties were found among the hog's head butter the following morning. It seemed John had found his secret elixir. Blanche was so ecstatic she let John sleep on the garage floor that night so he wouldn't have to go all the way to his usual doorway apartment that night. It was one of the loudest nights in the neighborhood, clearly memorable to the Peaches' neighbors. Some claimed it was a train, other more rural minds thought it was a dog caught in a bear trap. Of course, it was John Bickerson snoring. – ED.]

June 19, 1938

Blanche.
I can't stand it anymore.
Let's elope!
J

[This is where the main body of correspondence stops. At some point in the next six months, certainly before 1939, John and Blanche were married. Unfortunately, there is no known record of their marriage, either in City Hall — any City Hall in the United States — or in the Bickersons' papers. Jules Bickerson's theory is that John once went on a rampage, burning all the rice in the house, setting it on fire with Blanche's framed multi-copies of their marriage certificate. This is highly unlikely as it's a well-known fact that John never ate rice at all after he was married.

Like the last act of a flash flood, all letters between Mr. and Mrs. Bickerson stop at this point. There are several notable exceptions during the next 32 years, reprinted below, which come in the form of greeting cards mainly. As these greeting cards are cheaper, generic brands, there was no way of obtaining permissions from Crummy Cards, Inc., which has since gone out of business, for reprinting here. Obviously, all cards were from John to Blanche, with one notable exception as you'll see below. – ED.]

[Around 1944]

Happy Anniversary
to my wife
My life, my wife, my turtle dove
Life with you is great, it seems
I love you more than pork n beans

John

[Around 1954]

Dear Blanche,
What a life!
John

[Around 1959, probably upon the knowledge of Jules' impending birth.]

Dearest John,
Remember when we used to write letters like that? Like this? It's been so long! Why don't you write me anymore? Now that we're going to have a baby, I think we should try to make our lives more romantic again. Just like it used to be. Say you'll try, darling.

I was just thinking of our honeymoon the other night. You got drunk and fell in the potato salad. You were so cute! Little bits of pickle relish on your eyelids and when you opened your eyes, it all slid onto your nose. Of course you didn't open your eyes much that night, did you? Always nodding off before you even had the key turned all the way in the lock. Snoring all the way through our first dinner as a married couple. I had no idea you snored, John. Wake up while you're reading this, John! Come on!

Your loving,
Blanche

[1960 sometime]

Dear Blanche,
When I bought you that leafy fern, I didn't think you were going to use it as seasoning. I tell you there's no such thing as *sand* flavored!
John

[Around 1965]

Dear Blanche,

I'm writing to you like this because I knew that if it was shaped like this, you'd open it. *[No idea.– ED.]*

Where the heck are my shoes? If you've got them with you, don't you dare give them to Clara's kid, do you hear? I'll know if you did, Blanche! They always come back stretched so bad I have to use them as tire covers.

Call me!

John

August 1, 1973

My dear Blanche,

Here it is trash day again. I hope you enjoy the poem I composed for this very special occasion.

Roses are yellow
Flowers are too
When do we eat?
I'll be home at two.

John

An Interwiew with Jules Bickerson

What was it like having John and Blanche Bickerson for parents?
What's it like riding a bike on the ocean? I don't know. I've heard children of other famous parents who say that they grow up thinking that voluminous wealth and opportunities are normal, so they don't think much of living in a castle. But instead of wealth, power or fame, I was brought up in a loud household full of cats and dead bottles where I learned to sleep during the day and eventually pull my right eardrum completely out, a feat I'm still proud of to this day.

Wow, really? You only have one eardrum?
What?

What do you attribute to your parents' successful marriage?
……

I mean, how do you think a couple like that stayed together for so long?
A much more competent question. Obviously they really loved each other. They liked working for it. Much along the same lines as a wife who stays with her husband though he's always giving her black eyes.

Isn't that mainly from fear, that she stays with him?
There's a reason there's that term masochism. But usually it takes a sadist to complete the perfect couple. I think secretly my parents were half and half each, and they had that magic formula to know when the other one was the sadist, so the other could be the masochist, alternately. Of course they never actually physically hit the other, but sticks and stones, baby. Toothpicks and pebbles.

Your answers are quite thoughtful. It seems like you inherited your father's gift for intellectual eloquence.

I took psychology in college, basically to get a handle on who I was and why I started drinking at age six. I've been married more times than Buster Keaton plus Chaplin — yes, I looked it up — because I've always secretly been searching for my mother. Like it or not, I was unconsciously used to a shrew and I kept marrying nice girls. You know, the kind that wanted bad guys. But not the arguing sort, which I was. Guys with no knuckles and an expand-a-belly and tattoos running the length of his rock career. No one wanted to fight!

I guess I got restlessness from my father. But I don't snore and don't have trouble sleeping. From my mom I got an insatiable desire for thoroughly stinky food, like squid, and expensive hats. Both of which are a little difficult to explain to a potential mate. And I do try to run over every cat I can.

I was a psychiatrist for 6 years before finally settling on my movie usher career. I found the human brain exciting and stimulating, and thinking on it now, I was really just looking to hear others' fights. This was before the internet and reality TV made it quite easy, so I really wasted a lot of money and time on college courses. I just watch real TV now. Collect my disability from the ear.

Did your parents talk about having any more children?

Until they were blue in the face. But I never knew who was for what. It seemed like they were both on the same side, for or against kids, which makes it pretty impossible to have an argument, but they managed it.

I'm not sure what that means.

My mother had pets and I think that was enough. My father worked four full-time jobs during most of his life, so I don't think he had the patience, or life's blood, for an extra girl in the house. "Your mother is all I need," he'd say. "Am I really enough for you, John?" she'd ask, and he would sigh with, "*Plenty*." And the bell would sound and I'd go into my corner.

It couldn't have been all *bad.*

You're right. There was real love between them sometimes. Dad would offer Mom half the remote control every night after dinner. She'd get the volume and he'd get the channels. At least they were holding hands.

They once had a dog for three days. I remember that puppy. Half St. Bernard, half miniature poodle, with a bark like an upset sailor. This was 1970 and Dottie, that was her name, she got into the cactus Mom was raising for the milk she thought was inside. That poor dog yelled like an upset *fleet*, covered in those stingy things. They called an Irish doctor to come murder it, and as they took poor Dottie away, I was bawling and Mom was sobbing quietly on Dad's red flannel jacket that had been made from some old fireman's underwear. He kept scratching because when it got wet, it made it more itchy. He wanted to scratch, but didn't want to move her. I think that's my clearest memory of them. Quiet defining, when you head shrink it.

Why do you think the letters stopped after they got married?
You just answered that.

Do you think your parents are stars because they're typical, or a-typical?
Well, my dad was a humorist, you have to admit that. That man could think up more cleverness when his brain was 90% boiled in sleep deprivation than the greatest Jackie Mason or Jackie Martling in the world could craft in a month of Tuesdays. Obviously, he needed a great sense of humor to live with such a selfish woman. I loved her. But that was in my contract. He was drafted.

I remember their very last Valentine's Day together. Dad was working at a bakery, and Gaylord's, that's a department store, that particular day. Dog tired as usual. But still he managed to buy fudge covered ants at some Indian store. They'd mostly melted while he was on the evening job selling ties. But he trudged home, gave the cat a kiss and put the ants in the sink. Mom was waiting in her best evening dress which she'd got with his drug store credit card. He'd fallen asleep in the garbage can again. She was *fuming*. I went to my room. Locked the door. Turned *Bionic Man* up real loud, like I would always do. When it was on, of course.

Then it happened. Nothing. No sound. I turned down the volume, put my good ear to the door. Nothing. I opened up, and went into the kitchen. Dad was asleep on the couch in the living room/kitchen, just about to start roaring like the unabridged ocean. There was a red kiss on his forehead. I looked. The bedroom door was closed, the light showing underneath. She was probably reading.

I don't know if the impossible happened. No fight. It's one of those mysteries that will forever remain in my brain. Along with why people vote.

Do you think your parents are stars because they're typical, or atypical?

Definitely.

For the Best of The Bickersons

Bear Manor Media

WWW.BEARMANORMEDIA.COM